Wife Insurance

Wife Insurance

A WIFE-TO-BE NOVELLA

A'NDREA J. WILSON

Divine
Garden
Press

Published by Divine Garden Press, LLC
P.O. Box 371
Soperton, GA 30457
www.divinegardenpress.com

ISBN-13: 978-0692309247
ISBN-10: 0692309241

Cover Design & Interior Layout by Divine Lit Services
www.divinelit.com

Above all, love each other deeply, because love covers over a multitude of sins.

(1 Peter 4:8, NIV)

LIFETIME WARRANTY

Runaway Groom

I **don't trust women.** Not one of them. Not even my fiancée, Violet.

I know you're wondering why I am engaged if I don't trust my fiancée. I might not trust Violet, but I do love her, and despite the pain I've been through, I really want companionship. It's not Violet's fault—she's a good woman and she's never done anything remotely bad to me. If I have to point the finger of blame, without hesitation I'll direct every ounce of my disappointment, resentment, and animosity at my ex-wife, Sophia. I loathe this woman so much that the mere mention of her name causes my heart to race—and not in a good way. Most times, I don't even refer to her by her name. Instead, she's known to those close to me as She-devil.

I am on the phone with She-devil right now and she's complaining, which seems to be the only thing she knows how to do. In my mind, I keep trying to figure out how we went from being young and in love to complete strangers. I'm not the type to live with regrets, but until the day I die, I will regret the day I married Sophia Haven. And that's another thing. We've been divorced for almost seven years. Why doesn't she go back to her maiden name? Why must she hold on to my last name? I'll tell you why. She wants to constantly remind me that I'll forever be emotionally and financially shackled to her. Like I said, she is the reason that I can't be vulnerable to another woman, not even my sweet Violet, whom I've been engaged to for almost five years.

"I haven't received my alimony check this month, Cole. Why do we have to go through this each and every month? My check should be in my mailbox on the first. Not the second, the third, and definitely not the fourth. If I have to call you one more time about your delinquency, I'm going back to court and asking for more money. Or maybe I'll just have the judge arrest you for failure to abide by the terms of our divorce," she says in a whiny tone.

When I met her, the sound of her voice was soft and feminine, almost like a cool breeze on a hot summer's day. But now when I hear her voice all I can imagine is a pack of wild cats fighting over the carcass of a dead mouse.

"She-dev—I mean Sophia. I tell you the same thing every month. Payroll cuts your check and sends it out by the twenty-ninth of the month. I have no control over when the check hits your mailbox. I've pleaded with you to let them deposit the money directly into your bank account on the first of the month, but you won't do that, so I don't know what else to tell you. And as far as you taking me back to court, do what you want. Your little threats don't scare me. I've fulfilled my side of the contract. No judge is going to feel an ounce of sympathy for you when you're living in a five million dollar home that I bought and getting alimony checks every month that are more than some people make in a year. Get over yourself and get a job like everyone else in this world."

I hate the fact that she lives off my hard work and my money, yet still thinks she is entitled to nag me about the littlest things. As much as I want marriage and family life, I can't help but wonder if I'm doomed to misery if I ever truly commit myself to another woman. If nuptials to the first wife—who seemed to be everything I was looking for—turned out to be the worst decision of my life, will saying I do to Violet also be a big mistake?

She-devil sighs loudly. I guess she wants me to know that she's annoyed. I don't really care. "Whatever," she says. "Just make sure this doesn't happen again. Oh yeah, your son wants you to call him."

My son. Before I can respond, she hangs up.

I toss my cell phone onto the empty passenger seat next to me and refocus on getting through West Palm Beach's rush hour traffic on Interstate 95—I'll have to call my child later this evening. I am on my way to meet Violet and the minister at the church my fiancée has selected for our nuptials. By the time I walk into Pastor Harvey's office, I'm ten minutes late. His secretary ushers me inside and motions for me to have a seat next to Violet who appears calm and patient, as always.

"Sorry for my tardiness," I say to both people I've kept waiting. "Traffic was unbelievable."

Violet smiles politely. Pastor Harvey gently nods, then says, "Well, now that you both are here, let's talk marriage."

Violet runs her hands over her skirt to smooth it out. "Pastor Harvey, this is my fiancée, Cole Haven. He's the owner of Haven Hotels and Resorts. Cole, this is Pastor Ted Harvey, the new pastor of St. Paul's Chapel. He took over earlier this year when Pastor Scott died."

I reach out my hand to shake his. "Nice to meet you, Pastor Harvey."

He returns the sentiment. "Please, call me Pastor Ted."

"Okay. Pastor Ted, it is."

Pastor Ted leans back in his chair. "Cole, Violet tells me you two met five and a half years ago and became engaged after eight months of dating. Is that correct?"

I look at my fiancée and grin. She's beautiful both inside and out, and deep inside, I realize I'm lucky to have her in my life. "Yes. That's all true. I proposed to her on Christmas Day."

Violet blushes, then reaches over and squeezes my hand, which lies limply on the arm rest of my chair. "That's why it's so important that we get married on Christmas. When he asked me to marry him, the day felt . . . perfect, divine. We agreed then that we would get married the next year on

December twenty-fifth, but his son became severely ill and we ended up postponing the wedding."

Pastor Ted's eyebrows narrow. I can tell he is confused. Truth be told, it's my life's story and I'm confused. I'm not a mind reader, but I'm pretty sure of the question that he will ask next.

"So why didn't you all get married the next year or on another day?"

Violet looks over at me and lets out a hopeful sigh. "We really think Christmas is our special day and we want our anniversary to be on that day for sentimental reasons. The following year his company was expanding and he didn't have the time to dedicate to the whole wedding process. It seems like every year something comes up that forces us to push back the date."

I remain quiet. I can tell that Pastor Ted is doing the math in his head and the results are in—I've got more excuses than he has parishioners.

"I see," he says. "And *this* year? You both are committed to making the wedding happen *this* Christmas?"

"Yes. I believe so. I know that I am," Violet says, then glances over at me. "Cole, are you?"

It's the moment of truth. All eyes are on me. I want to just say yes and make Violet happy, but Sophia's annoying voice keeps replaying in my mind. God help me. "Well," I said, then clear my throat. "I . . . yes. I think so."

"You think so?" Ted and Violet say in unison.

I'm a businessman who knows how to be quick on my toes. Without much thought, I reply, "I'm just saying that life has sort of gotten in the way the past few years."

Pastor Ted's facial expression is blank, but I'm sure all sorts of negative thoughts are going through his mind—mostly about me. "Cole, Christmas is only two months away. If you two are going to have a wedding on the biggest holiday of the year, you'll need to start planning now."

Violet speaks up, taking me out of the hot seat. "Some of the details are already taken care of since we've had to call it off several times. I already have my dress, the guest list is made, the invitations, cake, reception hall, and whatnot are all on standby. We were previously going to use Pastor Scott to officiate the ceremony, but he's no longer with us. I know it's a lot to ask you to take time away from your family on Christmas to preside over our nuptials, but it would mean the world to us."

"Cole?" he says, requesting with his tone that I confirm our plans to make this Christmas the Christmas we finally tie the knot.

"Yeah," I manage to say. I peer over at Violet who looks so innocent and adorable. I've kept her waiting for five years. Marrying her now is the right thing to do, right? "We're ready," I say with a straight face despite the fact that inside, I feel as if I'm walking the green mile to my execution.

The Loveliest Flower in the Garden

Violet sends out the invitations. The cake is ordered and it appears as if all is in line for our Christmas Day wedding. Immediately after our meeting with Pastor Ted, I felt weak and frazzled, but now, two weeks later, I'm feeling more at peace with my decision. Violet and I have a wonderful relationship, and if I have to marry her to experience this kind of satisfaction on an everyday basis, well then I'm all in.

Today, we are having lunch at my Palm Beach resort with my best man, Robby, and Violet's matron of honor, Rose. Although the lunch is somewhat casual, we are also using the time to make final decisions on the reception, which will be held on the premises.

"I'm so glad you two are finally getting this whole thing over with," Rose says before gulping down her sixth glass of champagne. I'm not too crazy about Rose, but she's Violet's big sister and the woman who practically raised her. Their mother, Marianne, suffers from major depression and spent the majority of their childhoods in and out of mental health facilities. Over the years, she's become a bit more stable as medication to treat the disorder has improved, but I still feel uncomfortable being around the woman. Marianne's demeanor is somewhat stoic and melancholy. It seems as if the only bright aspect of her life is having four children, all named after flowers. Rose is the oldest, then Violet, their sister, Azalea, and the only boy, Delphinium, whom they refer to as Del. Despite Violet's crisis-filled upbringing, she turned out drama-free—at least I think so—unlike her siblings. Rose is an undiagnosed, functional alcoholic, Azalea has more mood swings than a mood ring, and Del has a woman in every city along the Gold Coast. I guess God, in all of His greatness, decided one of them had to be normal.

"Me too," Robby chimes in, then raises his glass—the third one. "I thought I was going to have to hogtie Cole and push him down the aisle in a wheel barrel."

Rose and Robby clink their champagne flutes together and laugh. I'm glad they're having fun on my account—literally.

Violet blushes. "Yes, I'll admit, it has been tough getting Mister Busy to slow down long enough to make me his wife, but all good things come to those who wait. Right, baby?"

She looks at me with puppy dog eyes. My heart melts. I really love this woman and can't believe I've been stupid enough to keep her in limbo for five years. "Right, beautiful," I say. "Thank you for being so patient with me."

I stare into her eyes. She stares back into mine and smiles. I feel like we're in one of those girly romance movies because some weird magnetic connection is pulling us closer together. When our faces are less than an inch apart, she whispers, "I love you, Cole."

"I love you, too," I say, and then close the gap between us, planting a heartfelt kiss on her lips.

"Uh . . . get a room! You know there are a bunch of empty rooms upstairs, and you own the place, so getting a key shouldn't be too hard. I'm just saying," Robby jokes, killing the moment.

Violet and I separate. I look over at my best friend since college and say, "Jealous?"

He shrugs. "I already have a wife, remember?"

"Now, is this the same wife that has kicked you out about three times?"

Robby laughs. "Correction, she kicked me out twice. The third time, I left on my own."

"And you think that sounds any better?"

"Not really. You're probably right. I might be a tad jealous. When marriage is good, it's amazing. But when it's bad . . ."

I finish his statement, reflecting on my own experience. "It's a nightmare."

"That's not true," Rose says with a slight slur. "I love being married."

"That's because your husband's never home," Robby reminds her. "Maybe that's the key to a happy marriage—spending a lot of time apart."

Violet grimaces and says, "That is not the key to a happy marriage."

"So, Miss I've-never-been-married-but-know-everything-about-marriage. What is the key to a happy marriage? Married folks would love to know," Robby says, challenging her.

Violet, not being the type to back down, crosses her legs and says, "Yes, I've never been married, and no, I don't know everything about marriage. But that doesn't mean that I'm completely clueless either, Robby. Marriage is what you make of it. Of course, every day won't be sunshine and rainbows, and endless happiness is not likely. But if two people are willing to commit to each other, work toward the greater good of the family, and keep the faith, I believe that a good and enjoyable marriage is possible. You don't have to avoid your mate like the plague just to get along.

"In my sister's case, her husband is in the military and his job keeps him away from home for long periods of time. In my case, I understand with Cole's hotels that he will also have to travel frequently and that may mean we won't get to see each other as much as I'd like. But when you care about someone, you compromise, especially when it comes to their dreams and what they must do to provide for the family."

Robby picks up the white, fabric napkin in front of him and waves it in the air as if he's surrendering in battle. "Violet, can you call my wife and explain that to her? Cole, you've got a keeper right here. Don't mess it up."

I smile. "I'm trying not to."

Robby's right," Rose says. "Violet has always been the sweetest flower amongst the rest of the weeds in our family. I always knew she would do well in life. Career-wise, she has done well, getting a college degree and now working at a university. Marrying a wealthy man is all that is left to give her the perfect life."

"Rose!" Violet scolds her sister, her face turning red. "I'm not marrying Cole for his money."

"You'd be the first," Robby says, snickering.

Hours later, I am relaxing in the Jacuzzi of my Palm Beach home, considering the conversation our small group had over lunch. Sophia had married me for my money. I didn't know it at the time, but I soon figured it out. I come from money—my parents own quite a bit of real estate and have stock in several Fortune 500 companies since the 60's. When I came up with the bright idea to open a chain of hotels and resorts, my parents were my biggest investors. It has only been a few years since I finally bought them out. As much as I appreciate their support, I want to have a business and career that isn't tangled up in their affairs. At some point, every baby bird must leave the nest.

Being surrounded by people with money my whole life, I'm not used to poor leaches. I've heard about people being taken advantage of for their wealth, but that wasn't going to be my story—until it became my reality. My parents warned me about She-devil, but I wouldn't listen. I was foolishly in love. Two years into the marriage, she was racking up bills that would be my downfall if I didn't cut her loose. My decision to divorce her wasn't just about her spending; the woman made it clear to me that her love for me was contingent upon what I could do for her, not how she could return the favor. I think that's why I fell so hard for Violet—she's given me much more over the course of our relationship than I've given her. With Violet, I haven't made all of the silly mistakes I did with Sophia. I didn't wine and dine her, buy her jewelry, or show her the full extent of my wealth until years into our engagement. I needed to make sure her motive was pure. She didn't even know that I was a hotel owner until after she agreed to marry me. Still, with all of the signs that Violet is the real deal, I worry that the moment we say "I do," her entire attitude will change, and I'll be left with another messy divorce and monster ex-wife.

Violet comes out onto the patio in flip flops and a terry cloth robe. As she nears the Jacuzzi, she slips off the shoes and the robe, revealing a simple, pink and black, polka dot bikini.

"Can I join you?" she asks demurely.

I am sitting in the middle of the built-in bench that faces out toward the ocean. I scoot over to allow her to sit next to me. "Please do."

She slowly sinks her body into the heated water and lets out a satisfactory "Ahh." Inching closer to me, she says, "Mmm. This feels so good. I really need a full body massage. This whole wedding stuff has got me in knots."

I nod. She's tackled a lot of the planning over the past couple of weeks and I'm sure it's been time consuming. "I'll send a message to Gigi to book you a spa appointment for tomorrow at the resort."

She leans back against the wall of the hot tub and closes her eyes. "You don't have to do that. I'm sure your assistant doesn't want to be bothered tonight."

I put my left arm around her shoulders, feeling like the ultimate alpha male. "It's her job, and I pay her very well to be available at all times. And it's my job to make sure my future wife is taken care of."

She shrugs. "Cole, I have a job. I can manage."

I look at her pensively. "Are you going to continue to work once we get married?"

She continues to relax—her eyes remain closed. "Of course I am. I love my job as an admissions counselor, and working at Palm Beach Atlantic University has been a godsend. The atmosphere is so peaceful in comparison to the schools I've worked for in the past."

I watch her like a hawk, looking for any sign of inconsistency. "But once you're my wife, you won't need the money. You'll move out of your cramped apartment and come and live with me, right?"

She laughs. She knows that I hate her small, one bedroom apartment off Okeechobee Boulevard. "Yes, I'm definitely coming to live here where I can enjoy this hot tub on a daily basis." She laughs and I stare at her mouth. I love to see her smile. Sitting upright, she turns to me as says, "Cole, my job is not about the money. Sure I need the money right now, and certainly, my financial status will be significantly upgraded when I become Mrs. Haven, but I don't want to give up helping students just because I'm married. I get the chance every day to meet wonderful people and to help some of them start the journey toward their dreams of getting a college education. You'll be working a lot and probably won't be home much. Instead of wasting time at the mall or watching soap operas and reality TV, I'd rather use my time to make a difference in the lives of others. Money or no money."

The words sound familiar, too familiar. My chest tightens a bit at the thought of where I've heard them before. "Sophia used to talk like that. She had these big dreams. She was going to go to school and get a degree in social services, then single handedly rescue all of the abused children in Palm Beach County."

"What happened?" she asks.

I sigh. The memories provoke unresolved emotions, even now—seven years later. "She married me and enjoyed being wealthy more than she did school. A few semesters in, she quit and gave up on that dream."

Violet twists her lips. I can tell she's thinking. She knows that I loathe She-devil and that a lot of my anger toward my ex is related to money. I haven't confided in Violet much about my previous marriage. She has asked me many questions over the years, but I keep my answers short and to the point—just enough to appease her inquires. I am aware that she wants to know more, but I am glad she doesn't press the issue. "That's too bad," she says after several seconds of awkward silence.

"It is," I say before allowing myself to drift away into thought about my past, present, and future.

LIFETIME WARRANTY

Switch-A-Roo

During our divorce, She-devil and I agreed to share our son, Tyler, on holidays. This year, I am supposed to get him on Thanksgiving and she will get him on Christmas. I honestly hate being away from my boy on any special occasion, but that is one of the consequences of divorce. Sophia has primary custody since I work and travel often. Ty comes to stay with me every other weekend, on his birthday, father's day, and alternating holidays. I am looking forward to having him for the entire Thanksgiving weekend. I've already lined up a few family friendly activities that we can do—"we" includes Violet.

Ty seems to like Violet. He's 9-years-old going on 29. When I first told Ty that I was going to marry Violet—five years ago—he said she was pretty, but she didn't look like a flower. He suggested that she change her name to Stephanie because that name fits her better. Five years later and he actually calls her Stephanie. I've tried repeatedly to tell him that isn't her name, but he refuses to budge. Violet thinks it's cute and answers to the name he's given her. I'm glad that they've bonded.

It's the Monday before Thanksgiving and I'm in my office at our corporate building in Palm Beach Gardens. I'm reviewing the numbers from last quarter when my cellphone rings, playing that old 1980's hit by Daryl Hall and John Oats, "Maneater." I've customized that ringtone for her calls only.

Letting out a deep sigh, I answer the call. "Hello, Sophia." I only answer because I'm supposed to get Ty on Wednesday and I want to make sure everything is in order for his visit.

"Cole," she says curtly. "There's been a change of plans."

I get that sinking feeling in my gut. She-devil is about to devastate me, again. "Oh no you don't. Don't even think about not bringing Ty to me on Wednesday. I have Thanksgiving this year," I say firmly.

Her voice softens. "I realize that, but I wanted to see if you'd rather keep him on Christmas instead this year. I know you're getting married on Christmas Day, right?"

"Yeah," I say, waiting for the catch. With She-devil there's always a catch.

"So I figured we could swap holidays this year, therefore, Ty could be in the wedding. He really doesn't want to miss the wedding, Cole."

Can it be? Is She-devil really being angelic for a change? Is she mature enough to put our differences aside for the sake of our child? Is she really okay with me marrying someone else to the point where she will grant my son the opportunity to attend the wedding?

No. Something is wrong. I've known She-devil for well over a decade. If she's being nice, either she wants something or she's up to something. Either way, I am getting ready to lose.

"So what's the catch, Sophia?" I ask.

She lets out a laugh that reminds me of a witch's cackle. "No catch. We just switch holidays this year. I'll pick him up before you leave for your honeymoon and you can come and get him on your next scheduled weekend from Tampa."

I freeze. What she is saying doesn't make sense. "Excuse me? Did you just say Tampa? Why would he be in Tampa?"

"Because that's where we're moving."

"What?" I ask, jumping up from my seat in the process.

"We're moving to Tampa, Florida. It's not a big deal," she says casually.

I begin to pace. I'm sure that my blood pressure is up—way up. "It is a big deal. Tampa's like three hours away. When is this move supposed to happen and why?"

"January first—well, actually December thirty-first." She pauses. "I need a fresh start for the new year."

I grab a pen from the top of my desk and fling it against the wall. I would have chosen something bulkier, but I don't want to alarm my executive assistant whose office is a mere feet away from mine. "You need a fresh start? You're moving my son to another city because you need a fresh start? That's ridiculous. Why don't you just be honest? You're moving to hurt me."

She cackles. "Everything I do isn't about you. My thoughts and decisions don't revolve around you."

"They don't revolve around our son either, do they? What about Ty? Have you even thought about how he will be affected? He'll have to change schools in the middle of the year, leave his friends behind, and be hundreds of miles away from his father because *you* need a fresh start." I feel my hands shaking. I'm so mad I could literally spit, but I'm inside my office and that would be unprofessional to do. Plus, the cleaning staff would hate me if they found saliva on their clean floors.

"I'm not going to argue with you about this," she says firmly. "I have the right to decide where I live. It's not like I'm leaving the state. I'm just not happy in Palm Beach anymore. I need a change of scenery. I figured you'd be glad I am leaving so you and your new wife don't have to worry about running into me anymore."

I'm adding up her words in my head, trying to make heads or tails out of them. Talking to She-devil is like playing a game of Clue—it's all about finding out what she wants, where she wants it, and what she's going to do with it. After a few seconds of scrambling my brain, I come up with the most logical explanation. "So is that what this is all about? You're upset because I'm getting married?" I ask.

"I couldn't care less about you getting married. Vain, aren't you? Anyway, my move is no longer up for discussion. So do you want to swap holidays or not?"

I grit my teeth. The woman is impossible. The discussion about her moving is far from over, but for the time being, I have the chance to include Ty in my wedding, so I'll take what I can get. "Yeah. I'll swap Thanksgiving for Christmas."

She says, "Mmm," as if satisfied with my response. "Fine. You've got him for Christmas. See, was that so difficult?"

I sit down in my chair, feeling exhausted like I've just boxed with the devil for twelve rounds. "With you, everything is difficult."

LIFETIME WARRANTY

An Indecent Proposal

"We swapped holidays. I've got Ty for Christmas instead. He can be in the wedding now," I tell Violet in response to her question about Tyler's whereabouts the Thursday evening at Thanksgiving dinner. Because I don't cook and I've never had a wife who could either, I always have Thanksgiving dinner at a fine dining establishment with friends or family. This year, Violet and I are eating at Dazzle, one of the restaurants inside of the Haven Palm Beach Resort.

She smiles. "That's great . . . that he can be in the wedding. He's nine so that might be a little too old to be the ring bearer. What do you think?"

I shake my head. "I want him to be up there with me. He can be my second best man; this way it doesn't throw off what you've already decided."

She pats my hand lovingly. "I don't mind making adjustments for Ty. He's your son, so whatever you feel is necessary, I understand."

I let her words float through my head. *Whatever I felt was necessary, she would understand.* I wonder if that includes my second thoughts about marriage. Probably not. Violet is ecstatic about this wedding, and I'm certain if I pull the rug from underneath her now, she'll be devastated.

Wiping the corners of her mouth with her cloth napkin, she says, "Was it your idea to switch the holidays? I'm surprised Sophia agreed, especially at the last minute."

"No, actually it was her idea."

"Really?" Violet says as a look of relief spreads across her face. "Maybe she's coming around. Do you think we should have invited her to the wedding? I mean, it might be awkward having her there, but I don't want to offend her by not extending an invitation."

A feeling of dread consumes me as I imagine She-devil walking into the church on my wedding day. "No! I don't want her anywhere near our wedding. I'm grateful that she's allowing Ty to attend, but Sophia always has a trick up her sleeve like this whole moving thing."

"Moving? Who's moving? Is Sophia moving?"

"Yes. That's why she's letting Ty stay with me for Christmas. She's moving right before the new year to Tampa. She claims that she needs a fresh start."

The reality of the situation seems to sink in and Violet lets out a fearful gasp. "Is she taking Ty with her? She can't do that."

Feeling defeated, I gulp down the rest of my sweet tea then shrug. "She can and she is. She has primary custody, so where she goes, he goes. I could probably fight it if she was moving out of state without my consent, but since she'll still be in Florida, there's probably little I can do. I can take her back to court for custody, but with my work schedule, no judge will side with me, unless you want to quit your job and be a full-time stepmother."

Simultaneously, Violet rests her right elbow on the table and her forehead against the palm of her hand. "I'm willing to do as much as I can to help with Ty, but I'm not ready to quit my job. Maybe in a few years when we have our own children, but not now."

"Well there you have it. Ty will have to go with Sophia until we can offer him something better. In the meantime, I'll have to figure out the best way to see him as much as I can."

She nods then reaches for a piece of pumpkin pie.

The remainder of our holiday meal is somber.

It's December 1ˢᵗ and I'm relaxing on my sofa, watching the news at the end of a long day. It's after 9:00 p.m. and I'm considering calling it a night when unexpectedly, my doorbell chimes. I absent-mindedly glance at my watch despite having just looked at the clock on the TV and knowing the time. My mind fills with all of the people who know my gate code and could have made it up to my front door without buzzing me from the end of the driveway. Violet, my parents, my assistant, Robby, and She-devil. That's the complete list. I walk over to the door and answer it, expecting one of the six.

It's number six, Sophia, wearing an especially skimpy bikini and a sheer sarong.

"Can I help you?" I ask as if she's a Jehovah's Witness or a uniformed troop selling Girl Scout cookies.

She offers a flirtatious smile then reaches back and places one of her hands on her lower back. "Actually, you can. I slipped and fell today, and my back has been killing me ever since. I'm sure it's nothing major, but I believe a nice soak in your hot tub will ease the ache."

I really don't like this woman. She's like a gnat that won't stop following you no matter how many times you swat at it. "Do I look stupid to you?"

Her smile disappears. "Of course not. Why would you say that?"

"Why can't you use the one at your house or at your gym?"

She cackles. "Because I would never use a public whirlpool and the jets in my tub aren't working. I was going to call someone to fix it, but since I'm moving and will probably sell the place, I figured I wouldn't worry about it. Please let me use your tub, just this once."

I let out a loud sigh. I really don't want to say yes, but I don't feel like this becoming an argument, or her throwing my refusal to help in my face a week from now when she decides to start seeing a chiropractor

for all of the so-called pain. "Against better judgment
. . . alright. But you've got thirty minutes. That's it," I
say inflexibly.

"Thank you! Thank you! I promise I'll be in and
out. I'll be so quiet, you won't even know I'm here,"
she says as she jumps up and down a few times. I
mentally note that her back isn't hurting that bad if
she can jump.

Despite her claims that she'll be quiet, I know
she's here. I try to block her out by going into my
home office to work, but she turns on the stereo out
by the pool, and the sounds of Kenny G's jazzy
instrumental version of "Silent Night" serenades my
home. I should have never let her use my hot tub, but
She-devil has a way of begging and pleading until
she gets her way, and I really wasn't in the mood to
hear the whining. I wonder where Ty is since he's not
with her, but I'm sure he's with her live-in maid-
nanny, Carmen.

At exactly minute thirty, I decide to end my misery
and make her leave. I stroll out onto my back patio
with a big white towel in one hand and her car keys—
which she purposely left inside my house—in the
other hand. She sees me looking like a poor excuse
for Jesus with both of my arms outstretched,
attempting to nonverbally communicate that it's time
to go home. She turns her head quickly, ignoring my
gesture and forgetting her promise to depart in half
of an hour.

"Hey," I say. "Your time is up. Come on and get out so that I can go to bed."

She shuts her eyes and leans back even more in the whirlpool. "I'm not stopping you from going to bed. I can lock up when I leave."

I raise my voice just a tad. "Oh, no you don't. You promised to be in and out, remember? I'm not in the mood for your shenanigans tonight, Sophia. Let's go."

She opens her eyes, looks out into the distance, and sighs. "I've been thinking about something while I've been in this tub."

I roll my eyes. "Yeah? That's nice. Could you please get out?"

"I've been thinking about how much I'm going to miss Palm Beach. I really love it here."

"You're the one who decided to move. No one is forcing you. If you love it so much, why are you moving?"

She looks directly at me. "Because of you."

"I didn't tell you to move."

"I know," she says. "I really don't want to move or make Ty change schools, but I just can't handle the thought of watching someone take my place."

"Take your place?"

"When you marry Violet, she'll be the new Mrs. Haven and I'll be a has-been. Even though we're no longer married, people still treat me like I'm your wife and I love it. I've always loved being in your life. You were the one who stopped wanting me around."

I hate melodrama and She-devil is notorious for it. "Please don't act like the victim, Sophia. You brought all of this on yourself."

She nods. "It's true, I made my fair share of mistakes, and that's why I don't want to make another one."

As much as I don't want to play her game tonight, I can't help but begin to add up the puzzle pieces. Call it a habit. "What are you saying? You're not moving?"

She sighs again. "I'm saying that I'm willing to stay here in Palm Beach if you don't marry Violet."

"What?"

"I don't care about you two dating. I'm completely fine with that. You guys can even move in together. Just don't get married. You've put her off for five years, why get married now? Just let things stay the way they are," she says confidently.

I want to be mad, but it's my fault for letting her use my hot tub. I knew she had a hidden agenda—she always does. "Are you out of your mind?"

"Not at all."

"You can't stop me from getting married."

"But I can move away with your son. Who's more important to you? Tyler or Violet?"

"Why are you doing this?"

"Because I like things the way they are. Because I don't want to be humiliated by this wedding. Because I don't want to have to face the happily married couple every day of my life living here on Palm Beach. Why don't you get that?"

"What you're asking is unreasonable."

"What I'm proposing is simple. You don't get married and Tyler stays here. You get married and we leave on New Year's Eve."

"Get out," I say, my voice a bit shaky. I can feel all of the resentment I have for her building up quickly. My blood begins to boil and I'm afraid that if she doesn't leave my presence soon that I might do something I will regret. "Get out!" I yell.

She obviously senses my agitation and quickly exits the hot tub. She grabs the towel and keys from my hands and speed walks toward the patio door. "Cole," she says once she's a good distance away from me, "my offer stands. I know it's not a perfect proposal, but it could work for everyone. Just think about it."

She slides the door open and leaves me alone, breathing in the warm night air. "Have Yourself a Merry Little Christmas" playing softly in the background.

LIFETIME WARRANTY

Wife Insurance

I **don't want to think** about She-devil's stupid proposal, but I do. I don't want to let down Violet again, but maybe I should. Possibly Sophia is actually right this time—for once. Things are decent the way they are, and getting married will only complicate my life more. Not only do I risk ending up in another bad marriage, but I will also be sacrificing having my son live less than five minutes away. Is making Violet happy worth all of this trouble?

One thing that's for sure is that I need to talk to Violet about my concerns. She knows about Sophia's plans to move, but she has no idea about what will make my ex stay. If Violet really loves me, she will understand why having Ty live in Palm Beach is so important to me, right?

Unable to keep the matter bottled up, I visit Violet's job at Palm Beach Atlantic University, unannounced. The school is located in downtown West Palm, right across the street from the intercostal leading to Palm Beach Island. I park my Jaguar in a visitor's spot near the administration building and rehearse my speech in my head during my walk to her office.

"There you are!" she says as she sees me walk into the admissions office. "I was just talking about you and poof, you appear."

She is smiling from ear to ear, practically glowing. A few of her coworkers surround her—all women and all smiling as well.

"I want you to meet Lisa, Carla, and Janiece. They'll be at the wedding, and guess what? They're throwing me a bridal shower next week. Isn't that so cool?"

I cough. I came to her job to let her down, but she's making it really hard for me. "Hello, ladies," I say, shaking each one of their hands. "Thank you for taking good care of Violet."

After a few minutes of wedding banter with the coworkers, Violet leads me into her office where we can finally be alone. I feel lightheaded. I want to be honest with her, but she's so excited about the wedding that she has everyone else excited too. I don't want to be the crummy fiancé that dashes her hopes and dreams.

"I'm surprised you stopped by," she says as she sits down across from me at her desk. "You never come by here. What's going on?"

I'm reluctant to spill the beans. My eyes widen as I feel overwhelmed by the stress of saying what's on my mind. "Uh, nothing. I mean, something, but I don't know how to say it."

She shakes her head as if she doesn't understand what I'm rambling about. "Say what?"

I take a deep breath and will myself to just spit it out. "It's just that Sophia came by yesterday and she's reconsidering the move to Tampa."

Her face brightens. "Really? That's wonderful. I know how much you want Ty in Palm Beach."

Okay, so she gets how important having a close relationship with my son is to me. I use her enthusiasm to tell her the rest. "Exactly. I really don't want to be separated from my son, but Sophia isn't easy to please."

Violet's smile drops. She's no fool. "What do you mean by that? What does she want?"

Tell her, I convince myself. "She wants us to delay the wedding."

Violet's eyes search my face as if she is looking for a hint that I'm joking. When I remain stoic, she shrieks, "What? That's crazy! We're not putting our wedding off for her."

I need to explain this the right way to her. I can tell that she's already offended. "Well, it wouldn't be for her. It would be for Tyler."

She jumps up out of her seat and places both hands on the desk in front of her. "She's just using him as an excuse to control you. Don't you see that?"

I nod. "Yes, I do. Sweetheart, calm down. I'm not saying that we're not going to move forward with the wedding. I'm just telling you what Sophia said. That's all."

"Cole, I know you love your son. I do too. I wish that his mother wasn't so controlling, but there is little we can do about it except not allow her to dictate our lives. We're getting married in twenty-three days and nothing is going to stop that, right?" Her right is more of a statement than a question. Her eyes narrow and I know she is expecting me to confirm that we're on the same page, but we aren't. Too bad I can't tell her that.

"Right," I say dishonestly. I'm too young to die inside of an office at a Christian college at the hands of my jilted fiancée.

Robby, who is supposed to be my best friend, laughs at me when I tell him about Sophia's proposal and Violet's reaction. We are playing a round of golf the next day at a local country club where we're both members. Robby technically can't afford to be a member at the Clear Lake Country Club. His salary as a lawyer is pretty decent, but the requirements at CLCC are excessive. I only joined the club so he could get in under my recommendation. I rarely hang out here unless he begs me to join him for a round of golf or Violet wants to meet Robby and his wife for brunch.

"I can't believe you told Violet what She-devil asked you to do. How did you think she was going to respond? She's a woman. They live for this whole wedding stuff," he says while lining up his shot. I watch him putt the ball into the fourth hole and pump his fist in victory. He's beating me so far, but it's not because he's better. I can't concentrate on golf when my life is a mess. After a sleepless night, I needed an ear to vent to and he needed a golf competitor, so I'm pacifying him with a game so that he'll hear me out.

Robby picks up his golf ball, looks up at me, and laughs.

"I know. I'm an idiot. Would you please stop laughing? You're not making me feel any better about this." I carelessly chip my ball twice before sinking it into the hole.

Robby snickers and replaces the flag-stick. He is still laughing as we begin to move toward the golf cart. "Sorry, but this is a classic Sophia move. I don't get why you didn't notice how evil Sophia was before you married her. I tried to tell you back then that she had ulterior motives."

"No one likes an 'I told you so.' But, yes. You did warn me. I was so caught up in her good girl act and model-like beauty that I was completely blind to what was really in front of me. I guess that's what makes me so uncertain about Violet. She also has that good girl charm, and although she's not as stunning as Sophia, she's still a beautiful woman. I don't want to fall for the same trick twice."

We climb into the golf cart and Robby starts it up. "Then don't."

"What are you saying? Don't marry Violet?"

He begins to drive toward the next fairway. "No. Get a prenuptial. That's where you went wrong with Sophia—you trusted her too much. You believed in this whole fairytale that you two would live happily ever after. And when she used you and then tried to take you to the cleaners, it took an army of lawyers to keep her from owning half of your empire. I know you have these ideal parents that never needed a legal, financial document between them when they got married, but people aren't like they used to be. Everyone these days is out for what they can get out of you, especially women. You're a rich man and you need to start acting like it. Protect yourself. There's too much at risk here."

"You think Violet would be cool with a prenup?" The moment the question comes out of my mouth, I regret it. Of course she won't be cool with it. She'll probably be insulted.

"She will if she wants you for you and not your money." Robby's perspective differs from mine. "I'm surprised you haven't thought of this before now. Aren't most wealthy people getting prenups these days?"

I nod considering all of the guys I've worked with over the years with young wives and airtight prenuptial agreements. "Many do. I just hate the idea of preparing for the end before we've even begun."

We arrive at the next fairway. Robby stops the cart and glances over at me. "Look at it like this—you have health insurance, home insurance, auto insurance, and life insurance. Why shouldn't you have wife insurance? That's all a prenuptial is—

hoping for the best, but planning for the worst, just like any other insurance policy you might have. In my line of work, I see too many people like you wishing they would have protected their assets. And those who get a prenup cry tears of joy when that simple document saves them thousands or millions of dollars during a divorce."

I raise my eyebrows in interest. "Wife insurance?"

"Wife insurance," he says definitively. "I can draw up the papers for you. Something standard so it doesn't seem like you're planning for divorce." He slides off the cart's leather seats and begins looking through his golf bag for the right club.

I remain seated in the cart. "Do you have a prenup?"

He laughs. "No, but that's only because I was broke when I got married. If it wasn't for my wife, I would have never gotten through law school or passed the bar. But your story isn't mine. If I were in your shoes, I would definitely have an agreement. But it's your choice. If you want me to put something together for you, just say the word." He pulls out his driver.

I sigh before getting out of the cart. I'm already tired of playing golf and hope that he grows weary soon. I can't help but to consider his suggestion of having a prenuptial agreement. Maybe he's right. If I get Violet to waive her rights to my money, possibly that will make me feel less concerned about whether or not the marriage will last. It's worth a shot.

I walk over to Robby who is now teeing up. "I'm not sure if Violet will sign it, but you're probably right. Wife insurance—I like that. How soon can you have it ready?"

LIFETIME WARRANTY

Moving On

Two days later, I am back in Pastor Ted's office with Violet. In order to marry us, we are required to attend six premarital counseling sessions. This is session number four. So far, the sessions have been decent. We mainly discuss our expectations of each other, our differences, our beliefs about marriage and divorce, and our faith. Although the first session started out a little bit shaky with the issue of us having a five year engagement, I think we've worked out that kink and have moved on.

"So Cole," Pastor Ted addresses me, "why do you think you previous marriage failed?" Well, I thought we had moved on, but to my dismay, the issue has resurfaced again.

I want to say, *Because she's a gold-digging demon,* but what I actually say is, "I don't think I knew my ex as much as I thought I did. It's not a matter of her changing during the relationship, which is to be expected to a certain extent. But she pretended to be someone she wasn't. Basically, I got duped."

"You think your ex-wife misrepresented herself before marriage?"

"Yes, I do."

"In what ways did she deceive you?"

The thought of it annoys me. "She pretended to be this wholesome, loving, caring, Christian woman who wanted to help people and make the world a better place. After we got married, she ended up being a manipulative, conniving, materialistic, selfish, money-hungry con-artist who only wants to bleed me dry," I say.

"And if you had known the truth about her, would you still have married her?" Pastor Ted asks, digging deeper.

I'd rather set myself on fire. "No. I love my son and I'm grateful that he's alive. But he is the only good thing that came out of marriage to She–I mean, Sophia."

Pastor Ted clears his throat, then asks, "Have you forgiven Sophia for deceiving you?"

When pigs fly. "No. How could I?"

He gives Violet a quick glance, but I catch their eye contact. I assume both of them are thinking the same thing, and I begin to feel like an outsider instead of her groom.

"How do you expect to have a good marriage with Violet if you're still harboring resentment toward your ex-wife?" Pastor Ted asks.

I don't like the direction of this conversation. Is it "Gang Up on Cole Day"? Did I miss the memo? "Violet isn't Sophia. One has nothing to do with the other," I say flatly, feeling a bit of resentment toward both of them. Violet may not be saying anything, but I can tell they're in cahoots. Pastor Ted doesn't know me well enough to pick up that my resolved issues with Sophia have influenced my unwillingness to commit, but Violet may have figured it out . . . and shared this concern with the pastor.

"I disagree," Ted says. He's been reduced to just Ted in my mind. "Yes, they are two different women, but once you marry Violet, both of them will have been your wife. How you feel about you ex-wife will impact how you treat your current wife if you do not make amends."

Let's stop the madness. "I thought we were supposed to be talking about me and Violet. I would prefer if we stop discussing Sophia. She's my ex-wife for a reason—we got a divorce. Can we move on to Violet?"

He sits back in his chair smugly. "That's a good question for us to end our session with. Can you move on to Violet?"

LIFETIME WARRANTY

Salsa Lessons

I am sitting in my office three days later giving my assistant, Gigi, instructions on what errands I need her to run for me today. Gigi has been working for me for the past twelve years and I think of her more as a good friend rather than just an employee. Because of our close working relationship, she knows almost everything about me from my clothing size to who is named in my will. She also knows all of the details about my bad marriage to Sophia and my current engagement to Violet.

"G," I say to her. "I need to ask you a personal question." From time to time with Gigi, I take off my boss' hat and put on my regular ol' guy hat, which is what I'm doing at this moment.

"Ask away," she says.

"How did you know that your husband was the right guy for you? How could you be sure that you weren't making a mistake when you married Quincy?" She's been married for fifteen years and it seems as if they have a good life together.

"Well, there really is no sure way of knowing. When you meet someone you really love, you just sort of have to take the risk. A part of it is being completely honest with yourself about the person standing in front of you. People are flawed so they are going to make mistakes. The question isn't if they will ever let you down, the question is, are you committed enough to this particular person to forgive them when they do."

I roll my eyes and say, "Here we go with the forgiveness thing again."

"Excuse me?"

"Violet and I are going through premarital counseling. A few days ago, the pastor was asking me if I've forgiven Sophia yet."

She chuckles. "Which you haven't."

I throw up my hands. People really don't understand. "I don't see what's the big deal," I say. "It's hard to forgive someone when they keep doing the same thing over and over again. The woman never stops. Anyway, what does whether or not I forgive Sophia have to do with me marrying Violet?"

She pats me on the knee. "Sometimes it's hard to give someone else a real chance when you can't get over what has happened in the past."

As much as I don't want to admit that unforgiveness is a huge part of my problem, I know they're right. But what if you really don't like someone and really don't want to forgive them? Forgiving means she could hurt me again, and that I've let her get away with what she has done to me. There's no way that I can pretend as if nothing ever happened.

I offer Gigi a crooked smile. "Maybe you're right. I don't know. I love Violet, I really do. I just don't want to make the same mistake twice. I just want to be one-hundred percent positive that marriage is the right move for us right now. I know there had to be something about your husband that gave you some level of assurance that he was the one."

She slaps her own leg lightly. "You know, there was something that happened that gave me a bit of confirmation. My grandmother told me that he was my husband."

"Your grandmother?"

"Yeah," she says with a slight giggle as if she realizes how unusual her confession sounds. "Sometimes older people have a way of knowing the truth. It's like they've got a spiritual gift or maybe they've just been around long enough to see things that younger people miss. But I'll never forget the day. It was the first time that I introduced Quincy to my grandma. We'd been dating for several months and I was falling pretty hard for him. He went with me to her house on Mother's Day and she stared at him for a long time, so long that he started to fidget. Eventually, she sent him into the living room so that she and I were alone in the kitchen. That's when she said to me, 'Thank God, I lived long enough to see your husband.' Of course, I told her that we weren't married. Then she said, 'You'll marry him. He's a good one.' I thought the woman was losing her mind. I loved Quincy, but we hadn't begun to talk about marriage. Sure enough, a year later, he asked me to marry him and I remembered what Granny told me. So I said yes. It was the best decision I could've made."

Gigi's words play over and over in my mind, leading to an unconventional idea. If older people really do have some sort of sixth sense, maybe I can use it to my advantage. Violet has met my only living grandmother a few times at family events, but Granny has never mentioned anything to me about our compatibility. Yet, the more I think about it, every time I take Violet near my paternal grandmother, Lucy, she is always surrounded by dozens of people. Possibly the reason she hasn't picked up a vibe was because there are too many distractions in the room. Then it dawns on me. I have to get Granny Lucy alone in a room with Violet.

The next day, I arrange to have Violet accompany me to visit Granny Lucy at the Palm Beach Shores Living Community. My grandmother is 85-years-old and smart as a whip. We arrive at the complex to find Granny Lucy poolside, taking a Salsa dance class.

"Move those hips, ladies and gentlemen!" the 40-something year old dance instructor yells.

I look over at the instructor who is peering at me and Violet as if we're messing up his class. We glance at each other, shrug, and join in with the class, swinging our hips back and forth to the Latin music coming out of a pair of speakers. I grab Violet by the hand and we dance our way over to Granny Lucy who isn't missing a beat.

"Hey, Granny!" I shout over the music. "How are you?"

She barely looks in my direction. "How do I look? I'm fabulous. Stop asking dumb questions, boy."

"I'm sorry. I haven't seen you in a while. I just wanted to make sure you are okay," I yell near her ear.

She continues to dance. "Okay, so now you've seen me and I'm okay. What else do you want?"

I glance over at Violet who is now *Salsa-ing* with a man wearing orthopedic shoes. She's no help at all. Turning my attention back to my Granny, I say, "I want to spend some time alone with you, Violet and I do. We want to tell you about our upcoming wedding."

"I already know about it. I got the invitation."

I need an excuse to get her alone. I should have guessed she wouldn't agree without a fight. "I know, but invitations are so informal. We want to tell you about it ourselves."

She huffs. "Don't you see that I'm in the middle of my Salsa class?"

My patience is starting to wear thin, but getting angry won't do anything but fuel her defiance. "I'm sorry, Granny, but it's not often that I get the time to come out here. I'm sure you'll have this class again next week."

Granny stops dancing and looks over at the instructor, rolling her eyes and gesturing with her head as a way to let him know that she has to leave his class because I've come to visit. The instructor narrows his eyes at me to express his disapproval. I flash him two thumbs up to communicate my pleasure in robbing him of one of his students. Violet's the only one who acts like an adult and mouths the word SORRY to him.

A minute later, we are sitting at a patio table with an umbrella overhead to protect us from the relentless Florida sun. We are close enough to the dance class to be able to hear the music, but far enough away not to have to yell over it when we speak.

Granny cuts to the chase. "So, what's so important that you're ruining my class? My instructor says that if I keep practicing, I'll be good enough to enter the Senior Living Latin Dance Competition in the spring. You're interfering with my training."

I take one of Granny's hands into mine. "I apologize, Granny. I just wanted to bring Violet out to see you one last time before we get married. Since the wedding is coming up in a little over two weeks, we wanted to come by and see if there was any marriage advice you could give us. You and Poppa Joe were married for over fifty years before he passed. I know you can give us some words of wisdom," I say before glancing in Violet's direction.

Violet nods and smiles. "It's good to see you again, Mrs. Haven. I'm with Cole. Any advice you could give us would mean a lot."

Granny looks back and forth between the two of us as if we're unruly children that can't be trusted. "So ya want my advice, huh?"

"Yes, Granny. Please?" I say sweetly.

Granny pulls her hand away. "Don't have any children."

"Huh?" I ask, confused.

"They make you fat, if not from childbirth then from eating from stress. I could have been a professional dancer if I didn't have your father and those other two stooges," she says unapologetically.

"Uncle Craig and Aunt Wynona?"

"Yep. Those are the culprits that stole my body, especially that Wynona. She was a big baby— almost nine pounds. I thought they were going to have to send a tow truck in just to pull her out of my uterus. After all of the damage she did, it's a miracle that my fallopian tubes didn't come on out with her."

Violet is now giggling and I'm staring at my Granny in horror. I've always known her to be a candid woman, but this takes the cake. "Granny, I thought you liked being a mother."

Granny sucks her teeth. "I didn't have a choice but to like it. My figure was gone, and your granddaddy and those children was all I had left." Granny looks over at Violet and says, "You're still young. Don't have any children, baby. If you simply have to have one, adopt."

Granny sits up straight and says, "Don't worry, I'll be at your wedding even though it is messing up my eggnog date with Mr. Bernard."

"Mr. Bernard who lives three doors down from you?" I ask.

"Yes. Speaking of that, can I bring a date?"

"You want to bring Mr. Bernard to my wedding?"

Granny stands. "Yes, so write me down for plus one. Is that all? I need to get back to my training."

"Just a second, Granny. Violet, do you mind meeting me at the car. I just want to have a quick word with Granny."

Granny huffs. Violet nods and politely says, "Sure. It's been nice seeing you again, Mrs. Haven. I'll see you and Mr. Bernard in two weeks."

"Hurry up, son," Granny says the moment Violet walks away. "What more do you need to say?"

Granny is still standing. I tug her arm lightly to get her to sit back down. "I want to know what you think about Violet. I hadn't gotten a chance to ask your opinion about this wedding. Just thought it would be wise to see what you thought . . . about her."

Granny scratches her head. "Can she cook?"

"Yes."

"Is her house clean?"

"Yes."

"Is she good in bed?"

I gasp. "Granny!" Who knew she could be so unrestricted?

She laughs. "Haven't tested the waters, huh? Well, if she's not, you can teach her. I'm sure that ex-wife of yours taught you a thing or two."

"Granny," I say firmly.

She senses my frustration and caves in. "Fine. She seems sweet. Doesn't matter what I think about her, you're the one who's marrying her. You have to follow your own heart. You might make a mistake like you did with that Sophia girl, but hopefully, you'll learn something from it."

"Granny, how do I know that I won't make the same mistake again? How do I know if she is really who she says she is?"

"After five years of being engaged to Violet, if you don't have a clue of who she really is, you might not ever know. Besides, she must be either very determined or super loyal if she's waited this long on you. Now, go on with your woman. I'm headed back to Salsa! Aye!" she yells as she speed walks past me toward the dance class.

I guess my granny doesn't have supernatural powers.

A day later, we are back in premarital counseling. Violet tells Ted about our trip to visit my grandmother. I'm still a little upset with the pastor so I continue to refer to him by his first name—in my mind. He seems pleased that I initiated the opportunity to have us visit my aging relative. His interest is even more piqued by the fact that we asked my grandmother for marriage advice.

"So what wisdom did your grandmother give you?" Ted asks.

I sigh at the thought of the embarrassing behavior that my granny exhibited yesterday. I really don't want to rehash the details, but both Violet and Ted wait patiently for my response. "She told Violet not to have children. Said it would ruin her body. I never knew this until yesterday, but my grandmother wanted to be a dancer. Having kids sort of got in the way of her plans."

Ted looks as if he wants to laugh, but he tightens his face and says, "Are you two planning to have children?"

"I would like to. Of course, Cole already has a son, but I'd like to have at least one or two of my own," Violet says.

"It sounds as if Cole's grandmother sacrificed her personal goals for the sake of her marriage. Are there career or other personal goals that you may have to give up in order to have a family, Violet?" he asks.

She bites her lip and chooses her words carefully. "We've talked about my job and whether or not I'll keep working. I like where I work and what I do. But I'm prepared to do whatever it takes once I have my own children. If that means leaving my job, then so be it."

"Cole, how do you feel about the idea of her giving up something she wants and enjoys for the sake of having a family with you?"

"I feel torn. On one hand, I make more than enough money to support the family, so I think it's better that she be with our kids than to leave them with a nanny. Yet on the other hand, one of my attractions to her is that she has her own career and isn't dependent on me for survival—unlike my ex-wife." I hate the fact that I just brought Sophia up in the conversation. As much as I dislike talking about her, it seems as if her name is never far from my lips.

Ted rubs his chin. "Before you married your ex-wife was she also self-sufficient . . . like Violet?"

Here we go again. We're talking about my ex and it's all my fault. I walked right into this one, so I have to deal with the consequences—I have to answer the question. "Yes and no. She was working, but she was much younger than Violet so her job wasn't really a career. She didn't make much money, but she had dreams of having a career and helping others. That dream never came to fruition."

"Why not?" he probes.

I shrug. "Once she got a taste of living in luxury, she no longer cared about working or helping others."

"Do you think Violet will change in the same manner?"

"Could be. Who's to say she won't."

Violet gasps. "Cole, do you really think I'll become like Sophia? You know I love being productive."

See, this is why I don't want to talk about Sophia; it just creates unnecessary conflict. I sigh and say, "I didn't say you'll be like her. I'm just saying that it could happen. It's one thing to hang out with rich people, it's another thing to actually be rich. Money changes people. It's a well-known fact."

I assume that she considers what I just said because she pauses, then quietly replies, "You're right. Money does change people."

LIFETIME WARRANTY

Slain in the Spirit

I enjoy listening to Christian radio when I'm driving in my car. The music is soothing and reminds me that no matter what I'm going through, God is with me. I need to know this truth right now with all the stress in my life. My wedding is exactly two weeks away and I'm still not sure if I'm really going to go through with it. I want to be with Violet, but marrying her means saying goodbye to Ty and that is so difficult to do. It would be cruel to pull out of the wedding at this point, but it's unfair to ask a father to choose between the woman he loves and his only son. I wonder, what would Jesus do?

In the middle of my chaotic thoughts, the song playing ends and an advertisement takes its place.

Come one, come all to the Winter Soul Revival at Greater Epiphany Baptist Church in Lake Worth this Friday! Be transformed by the teaching and prophetic word of Apostle Jimmy Paul McCoy. Need healing? Come! Need Salvation? Come! Need a word from God? Come! Whatever you need, God's got it, and the man of God will be in town for one night only to meet your needs. Doors open at seven p.m. and service starts at eight o'clock sharp. Come out and be blessed!

As much as it sounds like an advertisement for a sporting event rather than a church service, my interest is piqued. I need a word from God and maybe this is God's way of giving it to me. At the next light, I write down the information for the church that I've been storing in my short term memory. It looks like I'll be going to church tomorrow night.

I arrive at the revival at 7:45 p.m. I now understand why the doors opened at seven o'clock. The place is packed. The church is a decent size, but there are so many people that it's hard to find empty seats, especially for those who want to sit together. Luckily, I'm by myself so an usher leads me to an empty seat near the front of the church. I feel like things are going my way as I take my seat in the second row next to a woman in a large, decorative, pink hat. People continue to search for seats as the musicians take their places and the service finally begins twenty-two minutes later—not eight o'clock sharp like they said on the radio.

There is a praise and worship portion of the service which happens first. A team of seven people stand up in front of the church and attempt to get the congregation to worship God by singing several songs. I'm a little apprehensive at first, but after a while, I begin to clap my hands and sing along with everyone else. The lady with the pink hat next to me really gets into this part of the service, and from time to time she starts to do a little dance while shouting out praises like "Thank you, Lord" and "Yes, God." I have to admit that I'm amused. I've been going to church my entire life and have never seen such a display. My congregation is more reserved. We only speak and clap when told to do so. The idea of randomly yelling out whatever one feels is both alarming and alluring. For the fun of it, I try it out.

"Hallelujah!" I yell out then cover my mouth. It felt good to do it, and the best part is that no one looked at me weird when I did it. Instead, someone cheered me on.

"That's right, my brother! Praise him," the woman next to me says.

So I do it again . . . and again.

By the time the Apostle Jimmy Paul McCoy comes to the podium to preach, I am having such a good time that I'm a little sad we all have to quiet down. Nonetheless, I remember my goal, to hear from God if marrying Violet is the right decision, and quickly become excited again.

Jimmy Paul McCoy is a large man with an even larger voice. His booming voice seems to cause the windows to shake and the floor to tremble. The minute he begins his sermon, people start to leap out of their seats and cheer him on. Eventually, everyone is on their feet standing, so I stand too, despite not really being sure why. He is rambling about having faith of a mustard seed and miracles. I don't get how what he is saying applies to my upcoming wedding, but everyone else seems to love his words, so I go along with it and yell out a cheer too.

Then something unusual happens. Apostle McCoy leaves the stage and comes down to where the people are.

Isn't that against the rules?

The next thing I know, he's touching people's foreheads and they are falling out onto the floor as if they've fainted. He does this to several people and I can't help but wonder if he plans to do this to everyone in the building. For one, with the amount of people here it might take half the night, and two, I'm not certain I want to be unconscious.

Then Apostle McCoy starts calling people up to him, random people. He just points at them and they come up and he starts telling them things about their lives. Yet, the ending is always the same—he touches them and they pass out. I'm feeling a mixture of confusion, amusement, and fear. What if he points at me?

As if reading my mind, he makes eye contact with me and says, "Brother right there in the black blazer. Come on up here."

I point to myself and glance around me, seeking out anyone else who fits that description. "You, brother. Come," he says. I must be taking too long to respond because he calls for me again.

The pink hat lady next to me nudges me with her elbow, letting me know to get a move on. I slowly move out into the aisle and up to where Jimmy is standing.

What does he want with me? I wonder. *God, please don't let him touch me.*

Apostle McCoy begins to speak to me. "You have a faith problem."

Do I?

"You're worried about your life."

Yes, I am.

"You don't know what you're going to do."

Right.

"You're scared and confused."

Maybe a little.

"But God told me to tell you to be still."

Be still?

"Be still," someone behind me yells.

"Be still and know that He is God," Apostle McCoy says.

Ok–ay.

"You're worried about money," he continues.

Not really, but a little bit.

"You're tired of being broke."

Wait. What?

"You don't know how you're going to pay your bills."

Yes, I do.

"You're deep in debt."

No, no I'm not. What is this guy talking about?

"Be still and let the Lord fight your battles," Jimmy says. He's crazy and I'm forced to reduce him in my mind to Jimmy.

"Be still," someone yells out again.

"God's gonna work it out for you. Just be still. Be still," Jimmy says again.

Jimmy closes his eyes and goes to place his hand on my forehead, but I side-step him and he misses. He opens his eyes and notices that I've moved. He then goes to touch me again, but I duck, then I lean, then I bob and weave. He keeps coming after me, but I refuse to let him touch me. The people around me start to mumble. Jimmy yells out, "Be still!"

He comes after me again, but I back up. Before I'm fully aware of what I'm doing, I'm running toward the door. I think I've saved myself from being touched, but a thick security guy grabs me before I can get out of the sanctuary and holds me until Jimmy catches up.

"Now brother," Jimmy says, "I don't know what you're running from, but God says be still."

With that he touches my forehead, and everything goes black.

A Helping Hand

I don't know how Jimmy did it, but somehow he knocked me unconscious. The Christians around me refer to it as being slain in the spirit, but I'm not sure any spirit was involved—at least not the Holy Spirit. Jimmy's heavy hands and the excitement of the moment seem to be more of the reason than the Spirit. A few minutes later, I wake up to find myself laying on the floor in the middle of the aisle, covered by a thin white sheet. I sit up quickly and allow my eyes to dart around the room, assessing the situation. Jimmy has moved back across the room and is now focused on a young mother with two children. I throw the sheet off me, stand to my feet, and immediately exit the building. A few people try to stop me, asking me if I'm okay and if I need water, but I shake my head and push my way out of there. No more Charismatic revivals for me.

I realize that I'm being a bit extreme, but as the saying goes, desperate times lead to desperate measures—or something like that. I'm beyond worried about this quickly approaching wedding.

Christmas is only nine days away, which means so is my ceremony. What am I going to do? I'm still waiting for Robby to get the prenuptial to me. He says he will have it ready by tomorrow, and that I have to give it to Violet as early as possible. If I present it too close to the wedding day, it could be said that I coerced her to sign it by waiting until the last minute. She has to have enough time to make a clear-headed, informed decision to sign it. She also has to be allowed to present it to a lawyer of her choosing if she desires for legal advice and representation. With the clock ticking, I cannot afford to feel so indecisive. If I was only sure that this marriage would work, I wouldn't have to even ask her to sign a prenup.

In the middle of driving down Military Trail, I exasperatedly holler out, "God, help me! Tell me what I need to know! Should I marry Violet or not? Just give me an answer that I cannot deny!"

The traffic light in front of me turns from yellow to red and I bring my car to a full stop. I purposely yet gently bang my head a few times against the steering wheel. When I come up from my pity party to check if the light has changed, I notice a bright red lighted sign across the street. It's a business—a palm reader. I've never used a fortune teller before and I've always viewed them as nutty, but I'm desperate and I find myself thinking that maybe this is God's answer to my recent tantrum.

The light changes to green and I instantly change lanes and turn into the driveway of the palm reader's building. The place looks more like a house than a place of business, but beggars can't be choosers so I park and head inside.

When I walk into the door, chimes ring above my head, and I step into a foyer area. There is a sign on the wall that says to sit down, so I take a seat in one of the chairs nearby. In less than a minute, a middle age woman comes into the foyer and greets me.

"Welcome," she says. "I am Ananda. How can I help you?"

I start to regret coming into this place, but it's too late now. If I leave without speaking to her, I may offend her. So, I attempt to swallow my reservations. "Hi, Ananda. I'm Cole. I saw your sign outside and just came in on an impulse. Honestly, I'm not even sure if I should be here."

She nods. "Many people come on an impulse, but I see it as divinely led urge. What's troubling you?"

"How do you know something is bothering me?"

"Most people come because they seek answers for something in their life they don't understand," she says. Her voice is soothing and it compels me to want to know more.

"Yeah, I guess it makes sense. Well, how does this work?"

She smiles. "Basically, you sit down and I look at your hands. Based on what I see, I can give you some insight on your personality as well as things to come."

"And there's a cost, right? Not that I'm worried about the cost, but how much does it cost?"

"It depends on how much time and what you want to know. If you're looking for something specific, it shouldn't take more than thirty minutes. For a half hour, my fee is sixty dollars."

Her services are much cheaper than I assumed. I'm not sure if she can help me, but since I'm already here, I may as well give it a try. I dig into my wallet and pull out a $100 bill. I pass her the money and say, "Whatever this gets me."

She takes the money, puts it into the Fanny Pack that's around her waist, and says, "Come inside," and leads me into another room where there is a small table. I sit down at the table and she sits across from me. "Before we get started, tell me what areas of your life are you concerned about most?"

It feels awkward to tell a total stranger the details of my life. I decide that I'll give her the short version and let her figure out the rest. "I'm engaged and I just want to be sure that my fiancée is the right woman for me. I love her, but I don't want to have doubts if I'm going to get married."

She looks at me intensely. "A word of advice. You don't want to marry for love. You want to marry for the fate line."

"The fate line?"

"Give me your hands," she instructs and I obey. She turns my hands over so that my palms are facing upward. "Every palm has three lines that run across the palm—the heart line, the head line, and the life line. But there is a fourth line that runs somewhat vertically, and this is the fate line. This is the line that is most important, especially if you want to know your future." Although she hasn't asked me a question, she peers up at me as if she is waiting for my response.

"Yes, I want to know," I saying, listening intently.

"Good. If we look at your left hand, it will tell us about your past. But if we examine your right hand, it will tell us about your present and future. Since you're interested in marriage, we will focus on your right hand."

"Okay," I say, practically shoving my right hand closer to her.

"Mmm," she says as she studies my hand. "You are a very logical man, very analytical at times, and you're very cautious with your heart."

I nod. "Yeah, that's all true."

She stops assessing my hand and stares at me. "Love is a part of your fate; however, I cannot tell you if the woman you are engaged to is the right one for you. Instead, I can show you how to read her palm to know what to look for."

"Alright," I say, completely hooked and wanting to know exactly what to do.

She begins to point to a crease in my palm. "One of the most important things to look at is her fate line. You see how yours starts at the middle of your palm and goes up? You should marry a woman whose fate line is similar to this. You are more of a private person, right?"

"I can be."

She draws a line on my palm with her finger where there isn't a crease. "If her fate line starts at the edge of her palm and then curves up, marriage with her will be difficult because you are too different. She is very sociable which will interfere with your private personality."

She goes on to teach me several other clues that I can look for when looking at Violet's palm. I leave her abode thirty minutes after I arrive. Yes, I overpaid for the service, but I am content with what she has given me. I feel like I have something concrete that I can use to verify this marriage. It might be a little eccentric, but something is much better than nothing, and up until now, I've had nothing at all.

Violet and I have our final premarital session the day after tomorrow and I can't wait to get my hands on hers.

LIFETIME WARRANTY

If You Play Your Cards Right

At 10:00 the next morning, Robby casually walks into my office and slides a large manila envelope across my desk.

"What's this?" I ask.

He grins. "It's what you asked for—your prenuptial agreement. It took me a little longer than I originally expected because I wanted to make sure it was iron clad. I must say, I'm extremely proud of that document right there. It's some of my best work. Once Violet signs that agreement, you'll never have to worry about the future Mrs. Haven again."

I open the envelope and pull out its contents. There seems to be a lot of paper, more than I expected.

Robby must be reading the expression on my face because he says, "Oh, I made three copies of everything."

"Three?"

He laughs. "Just in case one of them mysteriously ends up ripped up. Women have a tendency to flip out at first, but when they come to their senses and realize what they are losing, they usually sign it."

I stuff the documents back into the folder and toss it onto the surface of my desk. "Thanks for putting this together for me. I feel awful that I even have to give this to her. A prenup was something we should have discussed when we first decided to get married, not now, eight days before the wedding."

"Probably so, but you know what they say— better late than never." He points at the folder. "Make sure you give that document to her right away. Don't procrastinate. Time isn't on our side."

I nod obediently. "I've got to meet with her and the pastor tomorrow for our last counseling session. I'll give it to her then—after the session. The last thing I need is her blabbing to the pastor that I gave her a prenup. I think she's been telling him about my ex. I'm not too crazy about the guy, but Violet loves him and wants him to officiate the ceremony, so I'm tolerating him."

"What's so bad about this pastor?"

I shrug. "I can't put my finger on it, but it's like he's a bit biased as if he already pegged me as the bad boyfriend from the moment I walked in on the first day. It's probably something Violet's confided in him about and he has a negative perception of me."

"Yeah, well look at it like this. After next week, you won't even have to deal with this man anymore. Anyway, what are you getting your bride-to-be for Christmas this year? My wife is still nagging me about that tennis bracelet you got Violet last year.

She wants one, but I have to keep reminding her that our last name isn't Haven," he says then chuckles.

I grimace. "Violet's already gotten her Christmas present. This wedding is costing me a small fortune and that doesn't include the honeymoon in Morocco."

"Big spender! Morocco's going to be nice." He steps closer to my desk. "So . . . it looks like it's going to happen. You're really going to marry her, huh?"

I let out a heavy sigh. "I think so, but I won't know for sure until tomorrow. Once I give her this prenup and look at her palm, I should know what to do."

He stares at me like I'm a madman. "Look at her palm? Why would you be looking at her palm?"

"I went to see this lady and she . . ." I start to say. "You know what? Never mind. It's a long story."

Robby walks backward in the direction of the door. "Okay. I'm heading to work, but let me know what happens tomorrow. Hopefully she won't deck you."

I laugh. "Keep a raw steak on ice for me just in case."

On my way home for work, I stop by Sophia's house to drop off Ty's tuxedo and shoes. There is a moving truck in the driveway and her front door is wide open. Usually I would knock, but I step into the house and begin surveying it.

Most of her belongings have been packed up into boxes that are spread out along the floor. Her walls are void of any paintings, pictures, or décor that were previously there. The only signs that someone still lives there are the sofas in the living room and the smell of takeout coming from the kitchen.

"Sophia," I call out into the house after being inside for a few minutes and not seeing her or Tyler.

Several seconds later, she enters the room, her arms filled with Ty's toys.

"What's going on?" I ask.

"You don't knock anymore?" she asks.

"The door was open. What's all of this stuff?"

"I'm moving, remember?"

I let out a sad sigh. "I haven't responded to your offer yet."

Sophia cackles. "Well since you have Ty's tuxedo in your hands, I'm guessing the answer is that you're still planning to get married. Am I right?"

"I don't know." It's the truth. I really don't.

"Stop playing games, Cole. Your wedding is in a week. If you're not going to go through with it, now would be a good time to call it off."

I can't let her leave like this. I can't let her take my son from me. I step closer to her and place my hand on her shoulder. "Is there any other way you would consider staying?"

She brushes my hand away. "No."

I feel like I've been sucker punched. I take a few steps back and attempt to regain a stoic demeanor. "I see. If you're not moving until New Year's Eve, why is there a moving truck outside?"

She acts as if she doesn't know that she's ruining my life, but I know she knows and that she's enjoying every minute of it. "I have way too much stuff to move at one time. I'm having movers take the majority of it now, so that when I get there I won't have to live out of boxes—it will all be set up for me."

"Oh," I say, feeling awkward and vulnerable. "Where's Ty?"

"He's down the street with his friends, trying to get as much time with them before we leave. I really hate to separate him from his buddies, but I guess that's a part of life."

I'm trying to contain my emotions, but the thought of Ty being separated from everything he knows is too painful to bear. "Don't do this, Sophia. Ty's life doesn't have to be this way," I say passionately. In a moment of desperation, I rush toward her, grab her hand, and flip over her palm. I quickly take notice of her fate line before she has a chance to withdraw her hand from me. As I suspect, her fate line starts near the edge of the palm, opposite of my centered fate line. I should have never married her. She has always been wrong for me.

She takes her hand back and smirks at me. "You're the one that holds the cards. I guess Violet means more to you than Tyler does."

Her words cut me, deep. "That's not fair, Sophia, and you know it. Ty is the most important person in my life, but I can't just walk out on Violet because you want to use him as a bargaining chip."

"Whatever helps you sleep at night, Cole." She turns and walks back out of the room. "You can leave the tuxedo in the hallway closet. I'll make sure that he gets it."

LIFETIME WARRANTY

Now or Never

I'm sitting in the final premarital counseling session feeling restless. I didn't sleep well last night, but how could I? It's exactly a week before my wedding and my entire life's in limbo. Half of my ex-wife's household is on its way to Tampa, including my son's bedroom set. I'm carrying a prenuptial agreement in my briefcase that my fiancée doesn't know anything about . . . yet, and I've been rehearsing in my mind what to look for on Violet's palm to verify whether or not she's really the right choice for me.

During the counseling, I keep trying to catch a glimpse of Violet's palm, but she keeps her hands folded the entire time. I find myself thinking that if I could only see her palms first, it might give me the confidence to marry her, or at least give her the prenuptial agreement.

"Is everything okay, Mr. Haven? You seem like you're somewhere else." Ted notices that I'm distracted and calls me on it.

I glance at Violet who is quieter than usual. She is also looking at me as if she's curious about my mental absence. "Sorry," I say. "Just have a lot on my mind with the holidays and the wedding and whatnot."

"I understand. It appears that we've come to our final session before the ceremony. You two are opting out of the wedding rehearsal since you're having a Christmas wedding and don't want to inconvenience your wedding party any further, which means that I won't see you until the big day. Are there any last questions, reservations, or issues that we should discuss?" Ted asks.

It would probably be the perfect time to bring up the prenuptial agreement, my exes move, and my fear of getting married again, but I clam up. The stress of it causes me to begin to perspire. My heart is beating double time, and if I wasn't in better shape, I would swear I was having a heart attack.

"Cole?" Ted presses.

"Huh? No, no, nothing here," I say quickly.

He nods slowly then turns to my bride. "Violet?"

She peers at me suspiciously, then says, "I think we've taken up enough of your time."

"Okay. Well, let's have a word of prayer that God will keep your hearts and minds as you all prepare for this important step," he says before bowing his head and leading us in prayer.

Less than ten minutes later, Violet and I step outside of the church into the humid South Florida atmosphere and I feel an instant surge of relief. Being under the critical eye of Ted is unnerving and I'm glad I'll never have to meet with him again for counseling.

Yet my feelings of relief are short-lived. I still have a major bomb to drop on Violet, so I shift my focus to the new challenge standing in front of me.

"Are you going back to work?" she asks as we walk down the church's front steps.

"More than likely," I answer.

She looks at me uneasily. "Are you sure you're okay?"

Without thinking, I stop walking, grab her hand, and flip over her palm.

"What are you doing?" she asks.

I quickly assess her finger tips, shape of her palm, and the direction of her fate line.

"Cole?"

A cold shiver goes up my spine as I notice her fate line. It starts near the edge of her palm, opposite of mine, just like She-devil's.

I didn't expect this answer. I begin to imagine a life with Violet that mimics my experience with Sophia. I lose my breath for a second and gasp to catch it.

Violet pulls her hand away, jarring me out of my dramatic moment. "Cole, what's going on with you?"

I glare at her. How could someone so beautiful be so dangerous?

I now know what I need to do. I reach into my briefcase and pull out a copy of the prenuptial agreement, passing it to her.

"What's this?" she asks as she starts to review the document.

"It's a prenuptial," I say brazenly. "I need you to sign it before the ceremony."

Her jaw drops. "A what? Are you serious?"

"Yes. As you already know, I have a lot of assets. I'm not going to repeat the same financial mistakes in this marriage that I made with my ex."

She laughs but not because she's amused. "Wow! Is this what all of the years of waiting has been about? Not wanting to make the same mistakes with me that you did with Sophia? You're afraid I'm going to take you for your money? I knew that you still had pinned up resentment toward her, but until this very moment, I never knew how much you really believe that I'm just like her."

"I didn't say you were like her."

She waves the document in my face. "You don't have to say it. It's written all over your face. The way you've behaved over the years, some of the crass comments you've made to me, the way you keep avoiding marriage. And now you spring a prenup on me a week before our wedding? You definitely think I'm her. Pastor Ted was right—you cannot be in a successful relationship with me until you forgive her."

The mention of Ted makes me see red. I wonder why she wants to marry me when Ted is obviously her ideal man. "That man doesn't know what he's talking about," I say with anger in my voice. "You think he's so perfect. He's only a man, Violet, just like me. But I'm sure you've told him all of my flaws and how I'm the bad fiancé that won't marry you. Well, here's another of my flaws to tell him. I want you to sign a prenup. My son is about to move to the other side of the state, and I'm choosing to be with you over keeping him here with me, but I won't do it if you don't sign that paper."

"Oh really? Glad to know exactly where I stand with you." Violet rips the prenuptial in half and throws it in my face. Robby was right about that backup copy.

She steps closer to me and jabs me with her index finger. "I'm not signing anything. You listen here, Cole. I've been a good woman to you. I've been patient and I've been understanding for five long years. I did it because I love you and I only wanted to be with you, despite your many flaws. But I'm not going to do this carousel ride with you another year. We are either getting married this Christmas or not at all. You're going to have to decide to trust me, or not. What's the point of getting married if you don't have faith in me?" she asks then takes a step back and throws her hands up in surrender.

"I'm done with this conversation," she continues. "On Christmas Day, I'll be here, at this church, in my wedding dress. If you really love me, you'll be here too. If you don't want a life with me, do me a favor and don't show up. But if you do come, come ready to give me your heart, your trust, and your commitment, not with a get out of jail free card."

She stomps away, leaving me behind with a prenuptial agreement that is now nothing more than litter.

LIFETIME WARRANTY

Making Amends

I'm a mess. I thought getting confirmation about marrying Violet would be freeing, but it has only made me miserable. Based on the palm reading, Violet is more like Sophia than she is like me. If I marry her, am I'm setting myself up for another disappointing marriage and disastrous divorce? A prenup would take some of the risk out of it because I wouldn't have to worry about giving her half of my net worth, but for some reason, the document alone doesn't seem as if it's enough to resolve my problems—not that Violet will sign it anyway. The real issue is that I can't get over how much Sophia hurt me and continues to hurt me every time she uses my son against me. Recognizing this, I feel stupid about the way I've treated Violet, yet I'm not sure if I should even attempt to salvage our wedding. I find myself wondering if all of this commotion has happened because deep down I'm really not ready for marriage with anyone.

After sulking for days, I find myself standing on the steps of the church on Christmas Eve. It's the last place I thought I'd end up, but for some reason, I feel led here. I walk inside and into the sanctuary. The decorations for the wedding are already set up and I have to admit, the place looks breathtaking. I feel myself getting choked up as I imagine how lovely Violet will look in her white dress. Can I really stand her up on our wedding day? Can I really move on with my life without her?

In the midst of my thoughts, I hear someone walk in behind me. I turn around to come face-to-face with Ted.

"Beautiful, isn't it?" he asks.

"Very," I say.

He stares at the violet and white décor. "It's the best wedding decorations I've ever seen. I wish the church could always look this glamorous, but that wouldn't be practical."

"Well after tomorrow, anything that isn't rented, you're welcomed to keep," I say.

"Thanks. Is there anything I can do for you?"

I sigh. "I could sure use some prayer."

He smiles. "Now that, I can do. Nervous?"

"Uncertain."

"I sensed that about you during our sessions. It seemed like you didn't know whether you wanted to get married or run for the hills."

"Can I do both?" I ask and chuckle.

He laughs with me, a little too loudly. "Probably not."

"I'm sure Violet's told you all of our wedding drama."

He shakes his head. "Actually, she hasn't. I've only spoken with her during our sessions with you. I don't like meeting with the bride or groom separately because it can sometime cause dissention. Plus, it's best that the two begin to handle affairs as one. That's what's needed if they're going to have a good marriage. Unity, working together, compromise, agreement—not picking sides."

I feel dumb, again. "I guess I had you pegged wrong. I thought you and Violet were in cahoots."

"You're not the first man to think his fiancée is telling on him," he says and lets out another hearty laugh. "It's your own guilt playing tricks on your mind."

It's time to be real. "I believe you're right."

"Is this about your ex-wife? Still haven't forgiven her?"

"Probably so and no. Even if I wanted to forgive her, the woman is impossible to deal with. It's like she enjoys making me miserable."

"You forgive for your sake, so that you can move on with your life. She may not ever change, but that doesn't have to keep you in bondage to her."

"I gave Violet a prenup after our last meeting. I wasn't trying to hurt her; I just want to protect myself. I have so much to lose if this marriage goes sour," I admit.

He looks at me as if I'm completely clueless. "What about Violet? What does she risk losing? Money isn't everything, you know. When two people marry, both of them have something to gain and something to lose. You're not the only one."

I blink twice. "I never thought about it in that way."

"Well, had you brought up this concern in counseling, we could have all discussed it, together," he says and pats me on the shoulder. "I need to get going, but hopefully, I'll see you tomorrow."

"Thanks, Pastor Ted," I say as he turns and heads out of the sanctuary. He's been upgraded back to pastor.

Later, I make two calls. The first is to Sophia.

"It's late. What do you want?" she answers.

"To forgive you," I say.

She laughs. "Are you drunk? Bachelor party out of control?"

"No bachelor parties. I've been there and done that. I'm sober. I just need you to know that I will no longer hold what happened between us against you. I can't stop you from moving or using Ty to hurt me, but I can pray for our broken family, that one day we both become better people for the sake of our son," I say.

I hope she will respond positively, but instead she says, "That's nice. Are you done?"

Some people never change. "I think so," I say.

"Good. Goodnight," she says and hangs up the phone.

The second call is to God. I've made a lot of mistakes, but I'm grateful that his grace and mercy is much bigger than my wrongs. We laugh over my fruitless attempts at getting assurance and insurance about my wife-to-be. From looking for a prediction from my grandmother and attending a prophetic service, to trying to see my future in lines on my palm and giving my bride a prenuptial agreement, I've done everything but what the good book tells us repeatedly to do—have faith.

LIFETIME WARRANTY

Amazing Grace

I **walk into the church,** dressed in a black tuxedo. It's funny because last week when I walked into this same church, I felt apprehensive. I wasn't sure if marriage was right for me and if Violet was the woman she said she was. Now, a week later, I am certain about both matters. I love Violet with all of my heart, and I want to marry her, not because it will make her happy, but because it will be the best decision of my life.

I head over to the bridal suite, which is a large parlor marked with the word BRIDE. The door is closed, but I can hear the voices of women speaking on the other side. As I move closer to the door, their words become clear.

"What if he doesn't show up?" I hear Violet say.

"He'll be here. He's a bigger fool than I thought if he doesn't recognize that you're the best thing that's ever happened to him," says another voice that sounds like Rose.

"Maybe this whole idea was silly. Why didn't I just cancel the wedding when I saw that he was making excuses not to get married? Instead, I'm standing here in my wedding gown and I might not have a groom. I'll be humiliated if he never comes. I shouldn't have given him the ultimatum," Violet says sadly. I hear her sniffle.

"You did the right thing. Yes, it was risky, but it was time for you to put your foot down and be honest with him. Cole has jerked you around for the past five years. It was unfair for him to propose to you and then never marry you. If he didn't want to get married, he should've never asked."

"I know you're right, but that doesn't change how I feel about him or how terrified I am that he's going to leave me stranded at the altar. Are his groomsmen here?"

"Yes, they're here. I guess that's a good sign."

"And his son, is he here?"

"Yes, I saw him a few minutes ago."

"Good." Violet becomes quiet for several seconds then says, "But you haven't seen Cole yet, have you?"

"No, not yet. I'll go and look again. It's going to be okay. He loves you and he'll be here. If you can't trust the man you love, trust God."

"Okay," Violet concedes.

I hear moving about inside the room and someone walking toward the door where I am standing, eavesdropping. I back away from the door and hide behind a wooden column. Rose exits the room, closes the door behind her, and walks down the hallway in the opposite direction of where I am hiding. I wait until she rounds a corner before emerging from my hiding space. Slowly, I walk over to the large oak door that leads to my bride. I lean against the door, mulling over the conversation that I just heard between Violet and Rose. I'm elated that she still wants me to be here—that she still wants to marry me. But it breaks my heart that I've hurt her so much—that I haven't been as good to her as she's been to me. She has a right to no longer have faith in me, to no longer believe in me. I hope it's not too late to make amends and regain her trust.

I take a deep breath in, mustering up the courage to face her. With determination, I knock three times on the door.

"Yes? Who's there?" she says with a sad voice. I can tell she's been crying. My heart breaks a little more.

I keep by back against the door, my head is turned to the side so that I can hear through the door. "Violet, it's me. Cole."

"Cole?" she asks, sounding surprised to hear my voice.

"Yeah, I'm here. I came."

She is quiet. I force my ear closer to the door, not wanting to miss any words she speaks. "If you don't want to marry me, you don't have to. You don't owe me anything," she finally says, her tone a bit cold.

I wish I could see her face, hold her hand, embrace her so that she will know that my heart yearns for only her. Yet, I am on the other side of the door and I have to plead my case from afar. "You're wrong. I do owe you. I owe you a lifetime of commitment. I owe you the same love and loyalty you've already given me. I'm so sorry that I've put you through so much stress. I never meant to hurt you. I was just so scarred by my past that I couldn't see how wonderful my future could be. In my mind, I kept comparing you to Sophia, but you're nothing like her and it was unfair for me to make you pay for her sins.

"Violet, I want to marry you today," I confess. "You're exactly the kind of women I need as my wife, someone who is beautiful both inside and out. But to be honest, I really don't know why you would still want to marry me, not after how I treated you. So I understand if you no longer want to go through with the wedding."

I hear her move closer to the door. Her fingernails scrape the wood of the doorjamb and I realize that she, like me, is also leaning against the frame. "Thank you for saying all of that. I wish you would have just told me your fears about marriage. We could have discussed it and worked through it together. That's what a marriage is about—working together to reach a mutual goal. The only way that we can have a successful marriage is if we are honest with each other and understand that it's not you and me, but it is us—two becoming one."

They say hindsight is 20/20. They're right. If only I had communicated with her five years ago, we could call this day our fifth anniversary instead of a reminder of all of the years wasted.

I quickly agree with her. "You're right and if you agree to make me the happiest man alive and marry me today, I promise to keep working on that us thing, for the rest of our lives."

She sighs. "Don't think you're getting off that easy. What about that prenup? Is that still a part of the equation?"

"No. I shredded it." I grin as I think about the desecrated document.

"I understand why you wanted a prenuptial. You have a lot financially to lose."

"Someone wise reminded me that there's something that you could lose that is even more important than my money. You're risking your heart. I guess I am too. There's no prenup for that."

"Yeah," she says, her voice now soft.

I push my body away from the door and turn to face it. "Unless there are any other issues we need to work out, I'd like to offer another proposition. Violet, will you marry me?"

She lets out a light giggle. "Of course. Are you sure."

"I've never been more certain about anything in my life," I say with a bright smile. "I do have one last question for you."

"Yes?"

I'm glad we've decided to move forward with the wedding, but I can't help but wonder why she has extended so much grace to me. "Most people would have just cancelled the wedding rather than giving me the option to show up or not. Why did you risk the embarrassment?"

"Because I believe in you," she says. "I knew you would eventually make the right choice. Yes, I got a little nervous today and thought that maybe I'd made a mistake. I hadn't. I know you and you're a good man. I think we both needed to be sure that this was what we both wanted. If I could proceed with wedding plans not knowing whether or not my groom would show up, and if you could turn down the chance to walk away from an unpredictable marriage, we obviously both want this."

I let my forehead rest against the door. I wish I could kiss her, but it's considered bad luck to see the bride before the wedding—not that I base my choices on luck or superstition. If anything, this experience has taught me that God is truly in control. "Thank you for having faith in me when I didn't even trust myself."

"So are you two going to do this or not?" a feminine voice behind me says. I turn around to see Rose . . . and Robby standing in the hallway mere feet away, both smiling. It's apparent that they've overheard the most important part of my conversation with Violet.

I wink at them. "Absolutely."

I am standing at the altar with my two best men by my side. Violet enters the sanctuary and time seems to stop. I lose my breath as she gracefully glides down the aisle that's been covered by a white carpet runner and fresh violet petals. I'm certain our guests are on their feet, but I can't see them. My vision remains on the loveliest person I've ever known, and I can't help but consider that fact that I almost ruined this perfect moment.

When Violet reaches my side, her father reluctantly leaves her with me, but makes sure to give me a facial expression that is both a threat and a promise. I respectfully nod at him to express to him that I both understand him and won't let him down.

Violet smiles at me and my heart melts. I knew she would be a beautiful bride, but being in the moment surpasses all that I've imagined. I gently grab her hand and raise it to my mouth, kissing the back of it. Before I can spend another moment indulging in my future wife, Pastor Ted begins to speak and I am forced to give him my attention. Twenty-five minutes later, he pronounces us man and wife. I pull the new Mrs. Haven into my arms and plant a kiss on her lips that leaves both of us smiling for the rest of the day.

LIFETIME WARRANTY

Feels Like "Haven"

Sophia, true to her word, moved from Palm Beach to Tampa. It took several months, but eventually her house—the house I paid for—sold and she was able to pocket the profits. She purchased a lavish home in Tampa using the majority of the money from the sale. Two years later, when Violet and I had our first child, a son named Chris, I took Sophia back to court for a fairer custody agreement. Violet was able to downgrade her position to a part-time admissions counselor who worked primarily with students from Southern Florida, which kept her from having to travel and freed her up to raise our child. The judge in my custody case agreed with my appeal, and now I get Tyler every summer, during winter break, spring break, and one weekend a month.

It's now four years into our marriage and Violet has just given birth to our second child, a daughter named Courtney. I am in my wife's hospital room, admiring my newborn when the nurse comes in and spoils the moment.

"I know you probably don't want to give up Baby Courtney, but I need to take her from you for about fifteen minutes or so. I promise I'll bring her right back once we're done."

Reluctantly, I let the nurse take my baby out of the room. I look over at Violet who has drifted off to sleep. Feeling a tad bit emotional, I walk over to her and kiss her on the forehead. "Thank you, sweetheart, for making me a very rich man," I say.

I realize that she needs her rest, so I slip out of the room, down the hallway and stairs, and out of the front door. I stand outside, sucking in humid air, thinking that if I were a smoker, now would be a good time for a cigarette.

"Hey, is the baby here?" I'm so lost in my thoughts that I don't see Robby approach me, holding a bright pink balloon and an oversized teddy bear.

I look over at him and grin. "Yep, and she's already a heartbreaker."

He pats me on my shoulder with his free hand. "That's wonderful. Listen, Cole. I never got the chance to apologize."

"For what?"

He grimaces. "For the whole prenuptial thing. I know it was my idea and it almost cost you a good woman. I'm sorry."

I wave his words away. "You're not to blame. You simply gave me your opinion. I'm an adult—I didn't have to take it."

"But if I hadn't planted the seed in your head—"

I interrupt him. "Let me stop you there. The truth is I was petrified of getting married, and I was looking for any excuse to sabotage what I had with Violet. If you would have told me to jump off a bridge, I might have done that too. Seriously, it's not your fault. It was time for me to be a man and to let go of my past so that I could embrace my future. I just thank God that I saw the light before it was too late."

"Me too," he says, sounding relieved. "So where's this heartbreaking baby?"

I nod my head in the direction of the hospital. "She's in the nursery. You want to see her?"

"What do you think? I didn't come up here to see you." He chuckles.

I give him a questionable glare. "I don't know. It's going to cost you to see her. What did you bring?"

He shrugs and holds out the items he is carrying. "I got a balloon and this stuffed animal. What else was I supposed to bring?"

I sigh. "You should have brought a daddy insurance policy because I can already tell that this little girl is going to be the death of me."

Wife without a Ring

Shawna Claxton couldn't care less about capturing the coveted promotion at her job or having a fulfilling career. There is only one position she wants and has waited her entire life to get—to be a housewife. Though her friends think she is old fashioned, her current beau, NFL kicker Andy Tate, loves the idea. But when Andy finally proposes—in an unromantic way and without a ring—Shawna finds herself engaged in a very public battle between getting the man and getting the bling.

Wife Next Door

Felicia Jefferson and Morris Bryson have been best friends since childhood. Morris has always appreciated Felicia for standing by his side through his bouts with a lifelong disease. At age 16, they made a pact that if neither of them were married by the time she turned 35, they would marry one another. As fate would have it, at 36, his chronic illness worsens and he attempts to cash-in on his agreement with Felicia, wanting to experience marriage before he dies. As much as Felicia desires to grant her sick friend's request, marrying Morris means breaking up with her boyfriend of two years and sacrificing her plans to marry for love. Is a lifetime of friendship strong enough to survive an unexpected proposal, sympathy marriage, and a life-threatening disease?

Wife for a Day

Isabella James and Myles Wright believe they have what it takes to succeed as a married couple. They have been dating for a year and can't wait to say their vows. However, their wedding plans are put on hold by Reverend Holley, a world renowned preacher who mandates that in order to marry them, the couple has to enroll in and pass Hard Knocks Marriage Boot Camp's Fully Engaged Weekend. Feeling sentimentally attached to Rev. Holley, the couple agrees to his requirements, unaware that the final and most difficult test during the weekend is a mock day of married life. With unexpected, real-life obstacles steadily being dropped on them, and feelings of frustration growing unbearable as the hours pass, will Isabella and Myles survive 24 hours of matrimony to prove their commitment, or will the marriage boot camp turn their forever into never?

About the Author

A'ndrea J. Wilson is the author of over twenty books, including the award-winning Wife 101 series. A'ndrea dates her writing career back to high school where she majored in creative writing at Rochester, New York's School of the Arts. After graduation, she pursued careers in psychology and education, earning a Master's degree in Marriage and Family Counseling and a Ph.D. in Educational Leadership. An avid reader, she could never shake her passion for books, which eventually led to her penning her first manuscript. Her continuously growing body of faith-based work primarily focuses on integrating her clinical background and interest in relationship development with fiction; however, she also writes supernatural thrillers under the pseudonym Janell. In addition to writing, A'ndrea is a college professor and the president of Divine Garden Press, an independent publishing company based in Georgia. For more information, please visit her at www.andreawilsononline.com or www.wife101.com